Our Little Cossack Cousin

F. A. Postnikov

Our Little Cossack Cousin

CHAPTER I

CHILDHOOD ADVENTURE

No, indeed, we don't sleep through our Siberian winters, nor do we coddle ourselves hanging around a fire, — not we Cossackchildren.

I was brought up in Eastern Siberia, in a Russian settlement, on the Ussuri River, about fifty or sixty miles from where it joins the Amur. These settlements, you ought to know, were first established in the year 1857, in order to show the neighboring Manchus where Russian boundaries ended. The first were along the Amur, the later along the Ussuri River. No doubt I owe much of my hardiness to the fact that my ancestors were among the involuntary pioneers sent here by our government.

The source of the Ussuri is so far south that in the early spring there is always danger of a sudden breaking of the ice near its mouth and a consequent overflow. Now it is strange, but whenever we children were forbidden to go on the river something would tempt us to do it.

"You mustn't go on the ice, Vanka," father said to me one day as he left for Habarovsk, the nearest big city.

I remembered the command all right until I met my chum Peter. He had a fine new sled to show me. It could go so swiftly that when he proposed that we cross to the Manchurian side, I said quite readily, "Whee! That'll be grand; it isn't far, and we can get back in no time!"

Peter was on the sled which I was pulling, when we neared the low Chinese banks of the forbidden river. They were not as near as they had seemed. It had taken us a full half hour to cross, although we ran all the way, taking turns on the sled. Suddenly Peter called out in a strange tone of voice: "Stop, Vanka, stop! We must run. Look! Hongoose!"

I stopped so suddenly as almost to throw Peter off of the sled, and saw three Manchurians on the bank. They were standing near their horses who had huge bundles slung across their backs.

"Why," I said slowly, resolved not to be frightened, "those are merchants."

"No," said Peter, his lips trembling; "they have rifles."

"Ye-es," I reluctantly admitted; "but see their big bundles. They are certainly traders."

"We had better run—" began Peter stubbornly, turning from me.

"You're nothing but a baba (old woman)," I said contemptuously, a tingle of shame covering my cheeks at the mere thought of me, a Cossack boy, running from a Chinaman. What would my father say, or my grandfather? Whoever heard of their doing such a thing? Yet, to my great surprise, my knees trembled as I recalled a scene of two years ago, when the brave Cossack Kontuska was found two miles from our village with his head smashed open, and it had been decided that he had been murdered by the Hongoose. Then, with a certain feeling of being protected, there also flashed through my mind a picture of the revenge expedition that the Cossacks had organized, and even of the Chinese horse that had been brought later, as one of the spoils, to my own home.

As we stood thus, one of the Manchus suddenly threw the bundles from off his horse, and, leaping on it, rode at full gallop towards us. I caught my breath, yet instinctively picked up a huge piece of ice, while Peter raised the sled into the air with both his hands.

It was a regular Siberian winter morning, dry and clear. The sun was still in the east over the high Russian bank, so that it fell full on the approaching Chinaman, as we called him. The snow flew out like sparks of fire from under the hoofs of his horse, accompanied by a peculiar crunching sound. When a few hundred feet from us, the Manchurian changed the gallop to an easy trot.

"How a ma?" he said, when he had come up, surveying us with a broad smile.

With a deep feeling of relief something made me recognize the fact that he had not come to slay but merely to satisfy his curiosity. I noticed the round red circular spot on his breast as well as the red ball on his cap. These, I knew, indicated that he was a regular army officer. With an awkward show of friendship he turned us round and round, touching our clothes, looking inside of our hats, and then said something which puzzled us. But when he had twice repeated, "Shango-shango," I understood that it meant that all was right, but whether it related to our clothes or to us, I hadn't any idea.

To show that I wasn't afraid, I shook my fist at him saying, "You are bushango."

He understood, and smiling good-naturedly said in broken Russian: "No, no, me shango too." Then, opening his fur coat and putting one hand under it, he pulled out something wrapped in a small piece of rice paper. This he opened. It contained a few cookies smelling of peanut oil, and these he smilingly offered to us.

I leaned heavily first on one foot, then on the other, while Peter looked sideways, unable to decide whether it would be proper to accept such a gift from a Chinaman or not; but tempted by a desire to show it to our parents, we took it shyly. "How interested mother will be," I thought, quite forgetful of my disobedience. Mother, however, never got a glimpse of the treat; every crumb was eaten long before we got half way back.

When I reached home, I found mother in a very nervous state of mind. Some one had spread the report of our trip across the border, and in her anxiety she imagined all sorts of terrible things to be happening to us.

No sooner did she see me than she put down my baby sister, who had fallen asleep in her arms, and embraced me. A moment after she still further relieved her wrought up feelings by giving me a sound whipping, and still later, after I had washed myself and had had my dinner, both she and my older sister listened with many questions to very minute particulars of our little adventure.

CHAPTER II

THE FIRST DEER OF THE SEASON

It was April. Winter was over, but the sun had not yet had time to melt the ice in our part of the river when the alarm was given that the Ussuri had broken loose a hundred miles above us and was rushing toward our village at tremendous speed.

This news was brought by an officer who had been sent to give orders that the river be dynamited at once to remove the ice blockade.

I was awakened that night by a terrible noise resembling hundreds of guns shot in rapid succession. My first impression was that the officer and his assistants were blowing up the ice, but I soon learned differently.

When I had dressed and come out, I could see that it was caused entirely by the breaking of the ice. All the village, including babes in arms, were already on the banks. It was not light enough to see the whole picture, but in the half darkness the moving white field of ice blocks resembled now a herd of mysterious animals, fighting among themselves, jumping on one another, and roaring, as they rushed headlong toward the north, or then again more like spirits driven from paradise, and making their way into the unknown with cries and wails, in desperate panic and fear.

We stood there for two or three hours watching the ice blocks, many of them three or four feet thick and hundreds of feet long, pushed out on the shore by their neighbors, to be in their turn broken by new masses of blocks. When the sun arose the picture instead of mysterious became magnificent. As far as one could see there was a moving field of blocks of ice, gleaming in rainbow colors, apparently changing shapes at every moment. Those nearest to us rushed with the greatest velocity, the middle blocks moved more slowly, and those toward the low Chinese shore seemed merely a moving stretch of snow.

I had just noted that the river which I was accustomed to see far below our high bank, now almost rose to its level, when I heard quick, excited exclamations around me: "Deer! Deer!"

I turned to where the hands were pointing and saw a strange sight. Several of the small deer that we Siberians called koza, were sailing on a big block of ice in the middle of the stream. A moment after every person was in motion, even the women running home for rifles. I remained with only a few old men who muttered: "The fools! How could they get them so far away, even if they should happen to shoot them?"

But the hunter instinct, or perhaps the strong desire to get this particular kind of food, made every one reject the apparent impossibility of getting the booty from this terrible roaring river, carrying everything so swiftly away.

The animals approached nearer and nearer. We could see their occasional desperate efforts to jump from one block to another, always to return to the big block which quietly and majestically flowed among hundreds of smaller ones, which pushed around it, now breaking their edges, now leaving a part of themselves on its surface.

In a short time the deer were directly opposite us. There were five of them, a big stag and four does.

Suddenly there was a rapid succession of shots around me from the men who had returned. The stag fell, killed, I afterwards learned, by my uncle who had aimed at it as being the most precious. Two of the does also fell, but the two remaining started on a wild race for the Chinese shore. One of them was obviously wounded, for after two or three slow bounds she was caught by the moving mass of ice and disappeared under the water. I followed the other with a certain amount of sympathy until it was nothing but a tiny dot, and then turned my attention to what was going on around me.

There was great excitement. An old Cossack named Skorin, was trying to stop his nineteen-year-old son and two others from the mad attempt to push a boat on to the stream, in order to go after the slain animals. These had been pushed gradually nearer us by the ice, and Young Skorin argued that it would be easy to get them.

I noticed that this dispute was being listened to by our friend Che-un, a member of the Goldi tribe, one of the native Siberian races, who had lived near our village as far back as I could remember. He was regarded with considerable kindly respect by the Cossacks as being the most experienced hunter and fisher among them. He had on, as usual, his winter costume which made him look like a bundle of fur. It consisted of a nicely made deerskin coat, deerskin trousers and boots. His dark face, with its flat nose, its sparkling, black, almond-shaped eyes, was all attention.

Old Skorin turned to him. "Tell this madman," he said, "that it is certain death to try to get into the stream now."

Without giving him a chance to reply, Young Skorin burst out: "Say, Che-un, tell father how I crossed during last year's flood."

The Goldi did not answer at once. Instead, he puffed two or three times through the long pipe which he always held in his mouth. Then, slowly pulling it out, he said brokenly, "Were it a bear, I might go — but for deer — no."

"Oh, come on," said Young Skorin persuasively. "If you won't, I'll go with Vassili here. Come on, Vassili," and, with a recklesslaugh, and without paying further heed to the protests of his father, he made a bound to his boat which was lying among others on the snowy bank.

All of these boats were of the light Goldi type, built from three very wide boards, one about two feet wide, at the bottom, the two others on the sides, and two small end boards, all well-seasoned, nailed, and caulked, bent to meet and generally raised at the bow. All the boards were well smeared over with tar. Such a boat can be easily carried by two men, or pushed along the snow or ice. At the same time its displacement is so great that five and sometimes six men can cross a stream in it.

When the two young men had pushed the boat over the snow into the river, Young Skorin took his seat in it while Vassili ran for two landing forks, a gun, and one oar. When he returned, Che-un suddenly changed his mind and joined the daring youths. This gave great relief to all of the

women, who were filled with anxiety as to the outcome of the boys' crazy
venture.

CHAPTER III

THE BOOTY SECURED

The boat was soon on the river, partly on ice and partly in water, and the struggle to reach the big ice block on which the deer lay, began. We saw the hooks of the young men flying now to the left, now to the right of the boat. Sometimes one end of the boat, sometimes the other, would be raised high into the air. Now and then, as the stream carried them further away, we could distinguish that it had become necessary for the youths to pull or push the boat across some ice barrier. As we strained our eyes watching them, it seemed to all of us that they could never reach their goal.

Noontime came, and I heard my mother's call to dinner. I was so hungry by that time, not having breakfasted, that I answered at once despite my desire to see the end of the adventure.

I had scarcely seated myself at the table when my father and Old Skorin entered.

"You must eat with us, Pavel Ivanovich," said my father. "You can't go home. It's too far. Besides, it's a long time since we've had a chance to be together."

We all understood father's kind intention of trying to keep the old man's mind from dwelling too anxiously on his son's uncertain fate. Besides, my older sister had just become engaged to Young Skorin and this drew our families closer together.

Old Skorin stepped into the room with dignity, took off his fur cap, and walking to the corner in which hung the ikon, crossed himself. Not until he had done this, did he salute my mother with: "Bread and salt, Anna Feodorovna," this being the customary greeting when any one is invited for a meal.

"You are welcome, dear guest, Pavel Ivanovitch," was my mother's hearty response. "Take this seat," and she pointed to the place of honor under the ikon and to the right of my father.

"Where is Katia?" asked Skorin.

At this question I looked around amazed to find that Katia was not in the room. I had never before known her to be absent at meal time.

Mother answered with a trace of discontent in her voice: "I don't know. The breaking up of the ice seems to have upset the whole village. Run, Vanka, and find her."

I left my place at the table with great reluctance, not daring to offer any protest in the presence of my father, whose military training made him insist on prompt obedience.

When I reached the river's bank, I saw my sister among those yet there. She stood shading her eyes, in order to still make out the now scarcely visible boat. Her face expressed a peculiar mixture of admiration and anxiety. I recalled that she had had a quarrel with Young Skorin the night before, which had probably led to the rash undertaking. Inexperienced though I was in such matters, I felt that this venture had somehow resulted in her complete forgiveness.

When she understood why I had come, her first question was, "Is father already home?" Learning that he was, she ran as fast as if her heels were on fire, so that I could scarcely keep up with her.

When we reached home the talk turned to the appearance of the koza, my father saying that it was a good omen, that we should have plenty of deer meat that season.

These Siberian deer always move in a succession of small herds, and are followed and preyed on not only by men but also by wolves and other animals. For this reason our cattle were always safe during their migration. At this time, too, we always had an abundance of deer meat three times a day. The skins were saved either to be immediately made into fur coats and caps or for future use. Often on account of the abundance of these skins many of them were sold to traders who now and then visited our part of the country.

Every boy in our village learned all about the habits of the deer in childhood, not only from his relatives but also from the members of the neighboring Goldi tribes, or from Manchurians who use the growing antlers as an invigorating medicine, considering it almost as precious as ginseng, which is also found along the Ussuri River. Sometimes they paid as high as two or three hundred rubles for a pair. I knew several Cossacks who made a fortune hunting deer. They were also profitable to keep as pets, the horns of the male being cut off every summer, when just about to harden, and sold.

We were just through dinner when a shout came that Young Skorin had been successful. We rushed out and met him bringing the big stag to our house. My mother and sister helped him skin it and cut it into four parts. Then I was sent around to spread the news that that evening there would be a big feast to which the whole village was asked, this to be followed by a dance for the young people.

Toward evening the guests began to arrive, many of the men dressed in old uniforms, many others simply in belted, gayly embroidered red, blue, and gray blouses. The older people seated themselves around the table in our house, while the younger received their share of the feast informally at our nearest neighbor's, greatly relieved at being free for a while from the supervision of their elders.

The meal lasted a long time. There was first the traditional deer soup of the Cossack, then roast deer, and finally an unlimited amount of coarse rye bread, milk, and tea. Vodka, too, as an especial treat, was offered to the older people.

When the table had been cleared and moved out of the way, the blind musician, Foma, with his fiddle under his arm, was led into a corner. The son of the head man of our village (the ataman), took his place next to him with a harmonica. The dancing began with the rather slow steps of "Po Ulice Mastovoi" (On the paved Street), and ended with the Cossack dance, "Kazachok," led by an old woman named Daria, and Old Skorin, followed by more and more active dancers, until it finally terminated in the dancing of the liveliest Cossack present, each newly invented stunt on his part producing an explosion of applause.

During the dance the house was packed with people. The greatest excitement prevailed. Men sober enough in everyday life, seemed suddenly to give expression to something wild in their natures. By midnight every one present was so exhilarated that he was either dancing or beating time. Even Grand-dad Matvei, who was said to be a hundred years old, kept time with the music by shrugging his shoulders and striking his feet against the ground.

All that evening my sister and Young Skorin were the center of attention, their engagement having been announced immediately after supper.

CHAPTER IV

A BIG CATCH AND NEW PREPARATIONS

One evening, later in the spring, when our rivers were entirely free from ice, and the banks were covered with green grass and primroses, Peter came suddenly into our barnyard with: "Quick! Get your spearing fork! There's fish in the grass."

Without a word, I made several leaps to the barn where my father kept his fishing implements, snatched a fork, and followed Peter in a race to the river.

Just before we reached the bank, Peter grabbed hold of my hand. "Be quiet," he said, softly. "Do you see anything?"

I looked on the slightly waving surface of the river and along the bank, but could see nothing out of the usual.

Peter let me gaze for a while and then pointing to a small inlet formed by a curvature of the river, where the water was very shallow and gradually sloped toward the meadow, whispered: "There!"

My eyes followed the direction of the pointing finger. The grass of the surrounding meadow was partially under water, only a few inches projecting above the level. Here something attracted my attention. It looked like a brown comb moving gently back and forth. "A fin," I whispered, more to myself than to Peter.

Hardly breathing, we stepped into the water which reached to our knees, and made our way toward the brown waving comb of the fish. I held the fork in readiness and tried to keep between the fish and the river.

When we were about three or four steps from the fish, it suddenly threw itself in our direction, and so swiftly that I had scarcely time to throw the spear. Then something struck me on the foot and I fell forward into the water.

"Hurry," screamed Peter. "Help me."

With my face in mud and water, I could not at first understand the situation. When I arose, however, and had wiped my eyes, I was mad with excitement and joy. The fish had not reached the stream but was on the sandy bank, half under water. Peter was pressing his whole body on it, trying to hold it down. It was a sazan, extremely big, weighing at least fifteen pounds, and it took us more than five minutes to subdue it and carry it to a dry spot. When this was done I let Peter hold the fish with his fork while I ran for a sack. In this we carried the fish home, immensely proud and boastful of our achievement.

When father returned at night, he expressed surprise at the size of our catch, adding that he had heard that day that the keta were expected soon. This produced more excitement, for next to bread the most important food of the Ussuri Cossack is fish, and particularly the keta, a kind of salmon.

When the keta came from the sea at Nikolaievsk, they are very fat but get thinner as they go up stream, it taking several weeks to make the journey from the mouth of the river to the source. The Cossacks have to be very active during the migration, for it lasts only a few days.

But father had still other news for us which brought the excitement to a climax. He had asked the commander of my brother's garrison to permit Dimitri to return home to help with the keta fishing!

The day following our big catch, all of the men of our village set to work patching nets, sharpening their spearing forks, repairing their boats, while the women cleaned and got ready all the different necessary vessels from barrels to frying pans. Father had brought as much salt from the town as possible, but it would only be sufficient for pickling a part of the fish; the rest would have to be smoked and dried.

While all the village were thus engaged, two horsemen were seen approaching. They wore tall fur hats, had swords at their sides, and guns over their shoulders. Their yellow shoulder straps and the broad yellow stripes on their wide trousers which were shoved into high boots, the silver inlaid handles of their nagaikas (Cossack whips), all indicated that they belonged to one of the active divisions of the Ussuri Cossacks.

Surprised exclamations of "Mitya!" "Phillip!" "Brother!" "Son!" were heard. I waved a red handkerchief at them, recognizing Dimitri's companion as

Phillip, a cousin of my chum Peter. When they reached the village, they leaped lightly from their horses and kissed and embraced all present, answering as they did so the questions and joshing remarks hurled at them.

I learned that they had come on a two weeks' leave of absence, and that even father had not expected them so soon. After the first greeting, he said reproachfully: "There was no need for you to hurry so fast. You might have killed the horses. Why, it's only yesterday that I saw you."

"Don't be grouchy, father," said Dimitri. "We walked half of the way. I am very well aware that a Cossack's first duty is to his horse; his second to himself." And as if to demonstrate this, he turned to where I was trying to climb into his saddle and said seriously: "No, Vanka, don't worry him now. He is too tired. Better loosen his saddle girths, take off his bridle, and lead him to the stable. Don't forget to put as much straw as possible under his feet. Don't get on him, or I'll never let you go near him."

Although discouraged in my expectation of a nice ride, I was nevertheless proud of my brother and his confidence, and led the horse to a shed which, as was usual in our village, consisted of three sides only, the fourth, to the South, being open.

At that moment my mother came running up. She had not seen Dimitri for more than a year, and she hung herself on his neck, laughing and weeping with joy.

Then the interrupted work was resumed. Dimitri and Phillip left us to change their clothes, but soon returned and joined heartily in our preparations.

Part of the men now waded out into an arm of the river until the water reached to their breast. Through this arm the fish usually made their way. Here two fences, separated by a space of about two hundred feet, were to be built, one to the Russian bank, the opposite one from the water to an island in the river. First, poles three or four inches thick, were thrust into the river bottom, about a foot apart, and then willow twigs interwoven between. The fences were then braced from behind with posts tied with willow ropes.

When these were finished and the men had come back to shore, a big fire was kindled. Standing around it, they took off their wet clothes and hung them on nearby bushes or spread them out in the sun.

Old Skorin then pulled a basket with eatables from under a stone, and also a bottle containing vodka (brandy), in order, he said, to keep them from catching cold while standing around naked after their icy bath. Although their lips were blue and their teeth chattered, they laughed and joked as they took it. People don't complain of things in our part of the world.

A decidedly cold wind now began to blow and I was sent to several of the homes for what clothes I could get. Without, however, waiting for me to return, they began to spread the fish nets which were lying in big bundles on the banks.

I soon came back with some dry things for the oldest in the party. For Skorin, in addition to an old army overcoat, I had a pair of long socks made of heavy wool by his wife. She had pressed them into my hand at the last moment, bidding me to be sure to see that her husband put them on.

Skorin received these with a show of scorn, mingled, however, with a satisfaction that he could not disguise. "My wife," he said, "is always worrying about me. If we Cossacks gave in to our wives, we'd all be very tender-footed." But I saw that he pulled on the socks.

Having performed my commission, I turned to where about four hundred feet of netting was already hanging on seven foot high poles.Men were at work on this, tying up broken loops and fixing weights to the lower parts. Long ropes were fastened to the ends. The work was done with feverish haste. When my brother and Phillip came running up, another bundle of nets of about the same size was unrolled, and the two set to work patching it, putting all the skill that they possessed into the work. When the call for dinner came at noon, the netting was ready for use.

Now a difference of opinion arose, some wishing to continue until all the nets were finished, others contending that after a hearty meal they could complete the work more quickly. Skorin who despite his age, was the inspiration of all present, sided with those who wished to remain, but when some one called his attention to the fact that Dimitri and Philip had not breakfasted, he surrendered, and we all hurried to our homes.

CHAPTER V

"THE KETA ARE COMING!"

Certain that there would be something extra for dinner on my brother's account, I ran on ahead, and as I ran I tried to guess what it would be. We would have, of course, the usual borsch (cabbage soup with plenty of meat, potatoes, and onions, and sometimes the addition of sour cream), buckwheat kasha (porridge), and the inevitable tea and rye bread. But what else? As soon as I burst into the room, I knew, for mother was just taking a big fish pie out of the whitewashed oven in the brick fireplace.

The others came in as I was clapping my hands with delight, and we all took our seats around the big table. We had hardly finished eating our borsch to which, following the example of my father, I added two big spoonfuls of buckwheat porridge, when the door opened and Sonya, Peter's sister, came in so nearly out of breath that she could hardly ejaculate the words—"The keta are coming!"

She might have said the enemy, so suddenly did we all spring to our feet and rush out shouting the news to all whose homes we passed. A few minutes after, our boats were in the water with the nets, and the men at their assigned places with fishing hooks, hatchets, and ropes. The women were not behindhand in coming, not merely to gaze at the river but to bring necessary utensils.

I had no especial duty assigned me, and so in trying to help everybody, I managed to be a nuisance. It was not long before I received a kick out of the way from my father, who was assisting Feodor carry a heavy net. This sent me several feet down the bank.

Nothing disheartened, I grabbed hold of a boat which my brother and Young Skorin were pushing into the water. But they worked so rapidly that I lost my balance and fell flat into the edge of the river. My brother caught me up by the neck, shook me angrily, and tumbling me up on the bank growled: "Stop putting yourself where you're not wanted."

I hardly knew what to make of such unusual treatment from Mitya. To hide the tears which were ready to fall, I ran as fast as I could to the top of the bank and got behind some trees from which I had a good view of the entire river.

Here I soon forgot how sore I felt. The fresh damp air was filled with the aromatic fragrance of opening buds and leaves. For a mile along the Russian bank, the river shone mirror-like under the bright rays of the Spring sun. Its surface was slightly waved by the wind, except in one place where there was a peculiar disturbance. Sharp waves and splashes and two rows of foam indicated the approaching advance guard of the keta.

Two boats were rowing desperately to their appointed places on both sides of the opening between the two fences. Two other boats had already gone to watch lest the fish should turn into some other arm. Suddenly the men in these began to fire shots, no doubt to prevent the fish from turning. Their maneuver evidently succeeded, for the fish headed directly to where the other party awaited them.

As they came nearer and nearer I grew so excited that I leaped high into the air and yelled wildly.

Although it was not a big school of fish, it covered more than two hundred feet. As it came to the fences there was a great disturbance, heads and tails and even the entire body appearing far out of the water. A few individual fish jumped as high as the very top of the fence. A very large number became entangled in the spread nets.

Because of the number of fish, it became difficult to get the water end of the net back to land, and, for a while, it looked as if the fish would escape, nets and all. The hard work of the men in the boats seemed to accomplish little. Finally Old Skorin, alone in his lightbaidarra, separated himself from the others, and pulled behind him the end of the rope, while the others exerted themselves to resist the pressure of the fish. When he reached the bank, he wound the rope around some trees which he used as a block, until he made a sufficiently strong anchor for the party behind. Two or three men came to his assistance, and gradually the far end of the net, filled with an enormously large number of fish, was brought on the bank.

A little behind this net was another net to get the fish that escaped the first. Many fish, however, went under both and were soon out of sight.

The whole village now gathered with vessels and sacks, knives and hatchets. The fish were picked up, killed, and carried to improvised tables, where a row of women and two strong men started to work at cleaning, salting, and packing them in barrels. The work was continued until the salt gave out late at night. The remainder were left for drying and smoking on the morrow. All of the work was done in common; later the fish were divided among the different families according to the number of workers in each.

The next morning everything looked gloomy and muddy, for there had been a shower during the night, and it was still drizzling. Happening to recall that the year before at this fish season the weather had been dry, I ventured to ask: "Isn't it foolish to try to dry fish in such wet weather? They'll get wetter than they now are."

To my chagrin and astonishment, all began to laugh, and Young Skorin remarked: "They are rather used to being pretty wet, I fancy."

As I turned from the laughing crowd, who, as soon as they had cleaned some of the fish, hung them on ropes stretched in several rows along the bank, I noticed that "Granny" Daria and her adopted son were watching the workers. I soon saw that they were not there merely out of curiosity but to pick up the spawn which they washed in a big tank and piled in a barrel. Later I was told that Daria had been the first in the village to prepare caviar for sale. That was the year before, when she made enough money to purchase a cow in the city. We all envied her this cow, for in comparison with our undeveloped Manchurian cows she gave an enormous amount of milk.

CHAPTER VI

TIGER! TIGER!

I must have been at least a year older when father came in one evening, his face full of serious concern. I had just been uttering peculiar yells to amuse my little sister, but at once became silent, anxious for him to speak. As soon as he had warmed his hands a little at the fire, he turned to me with, "You will have to go after the cattle, Vanka, and try to get them into the yard." Then, turning to my mother, he added, "A tiger was seen in the valley last night." Mother began to make some timid objections to my going out because of the falling snow, but father interrupted with: "Trifles! He's a Cossack!"

My mother knew too well my father's conviction that the same discipline that prevailed in the camp should be found in the home, to say more.

I confess that I did not like the task assigned me. As I reluctantly arose, my mother, trying not to betray her emotions, bade me put my fur coat over my blouse. When I had done so, she herself tied a heavy muffler over my cap, and then turning from me, pretended to be absorbed in getting supper. The anxious look in her eyes, however, had not escaped me.

When I stepped out of doors, I could not make out anything at first. The wind was colder and blowing stronger than in the morning, and I rubbed my nose, remembering the half frozen one with which I had returned from a trip on the river two weeks before, resulting in a swollen face and a disagreeable daily greasing with goose fat.

After a few minutes I made out the fences, and then the road, down which I stumbled, hoping to find our cattle clustered as usual, about a big haystack, half a mile from the village.

The sky, as is customary in Eastern Siberia, was clear and full of stars. The dazzling whiteness around gleamed as if covered with thousands of jewels. More than once a clump of bushes made me sure that the tiger was a dozen steps before me.

Suddenly a sinister sound broke the stillness. I half turned to run, when it was repeated, and I recognized that it was only a cracking of the ice in the river below me, so I continued on, relieved. Snow circles now began to form around my muffled face and the deeper snow creaked under my feet. Gradually, however, all sense of fear left me for a while. The spirit of adventure, the thought of accomplishing so difficult a commission, filled my heart with the determination to do it as well as though I were a full grown man.

I had gone less than a quarter of a mile when I began to make out several dark spots approaching along the trail. Soon I heard the bleating of a calf, who, evidently trying to follow its mother, was discontented that more attention was not paid to it.

"They have scented the tiger," I said to myself, "and are trying to get home."

For a moment I felt glad that I did not have to go further. Then it occurred to me that should the frightened animals unexpectedly see me, they might run away so that it would be impossible to find them again that night.

Quickly stepping to one side, I crouched down next to a little hillock. I was a moment too late, for the cattle stopped and stood motionless, gazing toward the spot where I lay. When they renewed their approach, their rapid trot had changed to a slow, cautious walk. It was fortunate that the wind was blowing in my direction, for they were soon in line with me. I scarcely breathed until they had passed, when I leaped up so quickly to follow that I again frightened them, and they started off on so mad a rush towards home that they were soon out of sight.

It was not until then that it occurred to me that the tiger might have been following the cattle, that even now he was somewhere near where I had first caught a glimpse of them.

Panic stricken, I grabbed up the folds of my heavy coat and ran along the trail like one insane. Once I stumbled, and it seemed to me that I felt the tiger's breath on my neck, that his claws were outstretched to carry me so far away that even my mother could not find me.

Then, with a hasty glance behind that saw nothing, I gave a leap forward and continued my run. At last I caught a glimpse of the light from our house, which was at one end of the village; and completely out of breath, I broke into the kitchen and sank to the floor.

Mother, greatly alarmed, ran up to me, crying out: "For heaven's sake, Vanka, what's the matter? Are you hurt? Is the tiger—"

Gasping for breath, I answered weakly, "Yes, tiger."

This produced a commotion. My older sister began to cry; my mother caught up the baby from her warm bed on top of the oven and kissed her, while father with one leap took his rifle from the hook and put on his ammunition belt. Then, taking me by the shoulder, he demanded: "Where was the tiger?"

I muttered something so unintelligible that his face cleared somewhat. He evidently perceived that I was more frightened than the situation justified. To relieve the tensity of the atmosphere, he said in quite a natural tone, "You're scared, Sonny, eh?" Then added briskly, "Shame on you! Take a lantern and follow me."

These words returned to me all my presence of mind. I jumped up and feeling the necessity of something being done, ran for the lantern, lit it, and followed my father who, enveloped in his fur coat, was already out of doors.

When my eyes accustomed themselves to the darkness, I saw that all of our cows were huddled together near the barn. We drove them to a corral surrounded by a seven-foot high fence made of tree trunks.

When sure that all were in, father closed the gate, and turned to another corral in which were the horses tied to posts. At first I thought that he intended to drive them into the corral with the cows, but soon saw, to my great surprise, that he had not only untied them but let them go freely out of the gates. He even went to a shed reserved for a highly valued stallion and let him loose.

"Why did you do that?" I ventured to ask him.

"I never heard yet of a loose horse being caught by a tiger," he replied briefly.

"But the cattle—" I began.

"They're different," he said, "they haven't the sense to know how to protect themselves. Besides, they couldn't run fast enough, anyhow."

As we moved about with our lanterns, our dogs and those of our neighbors kept up a continuous barking. At last we turned toward the house, my father remarking as if to himself, "The tiger is a good way off yet."

"How can you tell?" I asked timidly.

"Why," he answered rather impatiently, "don't you hear how the dogs are barking?"

"Yes," I said. "Much more than usual."

"More than usual," he repeated after me with a sarcastic emphasis. "You'll see how they bark if a tiger ever ventures near our house. But come, it's time to go in. I'm worn out. You go ahead, I'll follow as soon as I've closed the gate."

I skipped to the house, feeling very brave with my father so near, and listened to the different voices of the dogs as I did so. That of little Zushka, who belonged to our nearest neighbor, seemed ridiculous compared with that of our wolf-hound, Manjur. I whistled to Manjur who was about a hundred feet away. He stopped barking and ran up to me. Hardly had I begun to pat his head than he suddenly stiffened with attention, his hair bristling. Then with a ferocious bark such as I had never heard before, he disappeared into the darkness.

The moon, which had risen, made the surroundings quite visible. Turning my head, I saw my father some distance away standing perfectly still, his face turned toward the road, his rifle raised to his shoulder.

I also stood still, scarcely breathing, until he set his rifle on the ground. As he did so he glanced at the house. Seeing me he called out roughly, "What are you doing here? Didn't I tell you to go in?"

"Is it a tiger?" I said with teeth chattering.

"I don't know," he answered; "but do as you're bid."

I had to obey, and stepping in, soon cuddled myself under the heavy fur coat that served as my comforter. But though I lay down I could not fall asleep until my father came in and quietly but a little more slowly than usual, got ready for bed.

I heard my mother whisper: "Did the tiger come?" and father's answer: "I think so, but for some reason he went away."

"Will he return?" from my mother.

"How do I know?" came impatiently from my tired father, and I fell asleep.

CHAPTER VII

THE NIGHT ALARM

A few hours before dawn I was awakened by our dog barking angrily, yet with a peculiar note showing fear and disdain. I could also hear him leaping up and down in one spot near the very door of our house. Instead of answering barks, the neighboring dogs gave forth long and deep howls. There was such a noise and mooing of the cows in the corral that it seemed to me they must be trying to stamp or hook each other to death.

Father and mother were already up, and I heard father's deep command: "Get me a lantern."

As soon as the match was lit I saw him as he stood in his night shirt but with his fur hat on his head and a rifle in his hand. As soon as the lantern had been lit, he seized it and rushed to the door, putting on his overcoat as he ran. I arose hastily, put on my fur coat, grabbed the hatchet lying by the stove, and followed just as he cheered on the dog who ran before him to the corral, barking loudly.

As I came near I saw my father thrust his rifle hastily between two fence posts. A second later came a short flash and the report of the gun. But my father's curses showed that he had failed to hit the mark. At the same time, I heard a roar so terrible in its fury and strength and hate that I trembled so as to be hardly able to stand. Surely, I thought, a beast who can produce such a roar can swallow not only one but several cows at once. How brave my father seemed to me as, still muttering, he reloaded his old gun with another cartridge. But here something happened. The great beast holding a cow in his teeth as a cat does a mouse, jumped over the seven-foot fence of the corral and ran off into the darkness, pursued by our wolf hound. With what sounded like the Cossack war cry, father followed, while I, too, made my way some distance after, this distance gradually increasing on the snow covered trail.

We continued in this fashion for perhaps five minutes, when the dog changed his ferocious barking to a pitiful whine and a new shot rang out into the air, followed by a short roar. I stopped in the middle of the road, unable to go a step further.

I don't know how long I stood there, but it was until I heard Manjur returning. I could just make him out but oh, in what a pitiful condition! He was limping so badly that at times he simply dragged his body along the ground. Tears sprang to my eyes as I heard his cries and hurried toward him intending to pat him on the head. But when I tried to do so, my hand found itself covered with a warm sticky fluid which I knew to be blood. I could feel that his skin was torn, one ear gone, and his left front leg broken.

Helping the dog all I could, I returned crying to the house. As I stepped into the room covered with Manjur's blood, my sister Katia gave a scream, while my mother with terror written in her eyes, exclaimed: "What's happened to you? Where is your father?"

"I don't know," I answered; "but see what the frightful tiger did to poor Manjur."

Mother, somewhat relieved, but still trembling, now came up and helped me apply greased bandages to the torn ear and broken skin of the faithful dog.

While we were doing this, father returned. Slowly he took off his hat, then his heavy coat, and in reply to my mother's mute questioning look, said: "I believe that I must have hit him for he dropped the cow,—yet he got away."

"Is she alive?" asked my mother with anxiety.

My father shook his head. "Her neck is entirely broken," he said, adding, "I hardly think he'll return to-night. To-morrow we'll get him, for he's probably hungry and will hang around." Then he ordered me and my terrified sister to go to bed in order to get up early, and busied himself with poor Manjur.

Long after the light was extinguished, I lay awake thinking of the tiger, my father's courage, my mother's anxiety, the wounded dog, and the dear cow. For some time, too, I could hear the low voices of my father and mother discussing the preparations for the morrow. One name, that of Tolochkin, was mentioned several times. I knew of this Tolochkin as a wonderful hunter of tigers. I had never seen him, however, for he lived more than forty miles away, and was peculiar in his habits, keeping much to himself.

CHAPTER VIII

WHAT CAME FROM ATTENDING A SKODKA

The sun's rays were already brightening the room when I awoke next morning. I jumped up from the bench that formed my bed at night and looked around. The fire was burning brightly in the big stove, mother and sister were clearing the table. Father was gone!

Quick as a flash, it occurred to me why he was away. He had gone to a skodka, a gathering of the villagers who are always called together when there is a grave matter to be discussed. My lips trembled in my disappointment, for I had hoped to go with father.

I dressed hastily, and then grabbing up my fur cap and coat started for the door. Mother saw me and called out, "Where are you insuch a hurry to go, you foolish boy? You're not washed nor combed, nor have you had a bite to eat."

"I haven't time," I mumbled. "I have to go to the skodka."

Mother, despite the seriousness of the situation, burst out laughing. "Do you think you are necessary," she inquired, "to deciding what ought to be done?" Then changing her tone she said, "Hang up your shuba (overcoat), wash yourself, and breakfast, and then perhaps you can go."

My pleadings to depart at once were in vain, and I had to do her bidding. I forgot the disappointment somewhat, in attacking with relish the well-prepared buckwheat porridge, rye bread, and tea. The instant I was through, nothing could prevent me from running to theskodka.

When I reached Fedoraev's log house, which my mother had told me was the place of meeting, I found the front room filled with neighbors. Peter, who was at the door under the low-eaved portico, pointed out a tall, broad-shouldered man, with a heavy beard and bushy hair and brows, as the renowned Tolochkin. I gazed at him with all my might. "How many tigers has he killed?" I asked Peter in a whisper.

"Forty!" came the answer. "And you ought to see the bear and deer skins which I saw in his yard the latter part of January."

I turned to the man again. I had been told that he was about fifty years of age, but he looked about ten or fifteen years younger. I noticed that he did not say much except to reply sharply to suggestions and arguments.

"Why won't you come with us, Ivan Stepanovitch?" I heard the village ataman, the head man of our village, say to him in a slow, persuasive voice. "We need you to show our youths how to hunt tigers. They've got to learn. We lost five cows and a dozen sheep last year, and this one rascal alone can ruin us. We'll give you half the price of the skin."

"I don't care for the company, thank you; I prefer to hunt tigers single-handed." He paused and added with a peculiar sarcasm, "I'm really not needed." Here he arose and left abruptly.

For several minutes after his departure, no one spoke. Then I heard my father's voice: "Since he doesn't want to come, let him stay away. We're no children to need help. How many rifles can we count on for to-morrow?"

There came a chorus of "I," "I'm with you," "Count on me," and then quite involuntarily, I found myself exclaiming loudly: "I'll go."

To my surprise everybody found something amusing just then, for there was a resounding laugh. A man near the door faced me with, "Where is your rifle?"

I looked straight into his eyes and answered earnestly, "Last year my uncle promised to give me one of his shotguns."

Again there came a new and stronger explosion of laughter. What was the matter? Were they laughing at me?

My uncle came to my rescue. "Brave boy," he said, patting me on the shoulder. "I'll take you if your father consents, and you shall have a rifle instead of a shotgun. We need some one to see to our horses."

Then the meeting began to discuss plans. It was decided that about two hours after midnight all who were going were to meet outside of the village at the crossing of the road to Bear Valley. Only two dogs, wolf hounds owned by Laddeef, were to be taken.

When I returned home, I said nothing to my mother of my share in the skodka, but when shortly after midnight I heard my father's heavy steps go out to feed the horses, I arose quietly and dressed, not forgetting my fur overcoat and cap and my warm felt boots. When my father returned, his beard white with frost and snow on his deerskin boots, he looked at me with a mingling of surprise and satisfaction and exclaimed: "You up! What's the matter?"

"You seemed willing that I should go on the hunt," I stammered, fearful of a refusal at the last moment.

"Seemed willing," my father repeated with a slight smile.

Here my mother who was now up, broke in quite excitedly: "You are surely not going to be so crazy as to let Vanka go."

That saved me. Father always disliked any interference, and now, in addition, mother's tone angered him.

"Father," I begged, before he could speak, "mother thinks I'm a baby. She doesn't understand that I'm to be raised like a Cossack and not like a lamb. Uncle will take care of me."

My father who was frowning deeply, seemed to be turning over something in his mind. At last, without looking at me, he said, "It'll do you good. If your uncle will take charge of you, — go."

I didn't give my mother a chance to utter a word but flew out of the door like a bullet, forgetting even to close the door after me, a negligence usually punished in our village by a beating.

I did not lessen my speed until I found myself at my uncle's felt-padded door. Turning the knob (it was not customary to lock doors or to knock in our village), I walked in. Uncle was still in bed and at first could not understand my presence. When he did, he jumped to his feet with "You rascal, you caught me this time, all right! Take any rifle you want."

He pointed to several antlers on the wall on which hung an array of rifles and daggers. While I tried to decide on the rifle, he washed and dressed, made a fire and began to prepare pancakes and tea. Having decided what gun I wanted, I helped him by hammering odd-shaped lumps of sugar from a big cone-shaped loaf.

From time to time he looked smilingly at me and uttered unrelated ejaculations, from which I learned that he favored my going.

We sat down, I thinking what a cheerful man he was.

"I guess you haven't breakfasted," he said, filling my plate. "Your mother probably gave you a spanking instead of something to eat."

I looked up at him in surprise. How could he know that I hadn't had anything to eat, and that my mother was angry.

Having eaten heartily, we went out. I helped saddle his horse, and then together, laughing and talking, we hitched a mule to a sleigh into which we put hay and grain, a bag of tobacco, some bread, salt and meat, sugar and tea, an arkan (the Cossack's lassoo), and some cartridges. I tried to follow his excellent method of packing things away neatly, for I knew that that was a part of the training of every Cossack.

When we were ready to start, I in front, he a few steps behind, his pipe in his mouth, a smile on his lips, I could not help asking: "Uncle, what are you smiling at?"

"At you!" he answered unexpectedly. "I guess you wouldn't go home just now even for ten rubles."

"Why—" I began and stopped, wondering again how he could read my thoughts. For it had just occurred to me that if, for any reason, I had to return, mother wouldn't let me out again, and perhaps even father— At this point, I hit the mule on whose back I was mounted, and we started off.

CHAPTER IX

THE HUNT

When we reached the meeting-place, more than a dozen men on horseback were already there. Close to them stood a big shallow sleigh, the runners of which were a pair of birch poles. In it were ropes, a hatchet, food and forage. The driver of this was Daria, an old woman, whom I have already mentioned once or twice. I knew her story. The death of her husband and two children of typhoid fever had caused her to be despondent for several years. Then some one left a foundling at her door. She adopted the child, trying in every way to make a worthy man of him. To do this, she accepted all kinds of odd jobs, even such as were generally given to men. She built fences, prepared the dead for burial, acted as midwife and nurse, delivered messages that nobody else cared to undertake, sometimes at night or during severe storms. She seemed to be afraid of nothing in the world and of nobody.

When she first began to work in this way, she was pitied and helped; a little later, she was laughed at, and unpleasant names were applied to her; but finally, all came to have a deep respect for her and to rely on her help when trouble came.

Long years of humiliation and struggle for a living, and the overcoming of all obstacles, had made her somewhat imperative in manner. She always expressed a decided opinion. Many people thought she really knew everything, and one or two superstitious persons even insinuated that she was a witch. When money or its equivalent in milk, eggs or flour was offered for her services, she accepted itfrom those who could pay. From others she refused everything, giving instead something from her own small store.

I thought her very odd, but liked her. Nevertheless, to-day, — well, to-day, it seemed to me that it was not fitting that I, a Cossack, should have to remain in the rear with a woman.

Comforting myself with the knowledge that Daria was a very unusual woman, I bade her good morning.

"Good morning, you rascal," she answered. "What are you doing here? I know that your mother is worrying about you."

I did not think that this needed a reply. Jumping down from the mule but holding on to the reins, I joined a group of Cossacks who formed a circle in front of their horses.

"I guess we're all here," remarked Mikhailov, an active, talkative fellow who had lately returned from actual service with the rank ofnon-commissioned officer and with the unpopular habit of constantly assuming leadership. He was probably the youngest present.

"Yes," replied my father. "And now we must follow some system. Perhaps we'd better cast lots to see who is to be our ataman, the leader of our band."

Old Skorin shook his head. "What's the use of that?" he said. "You know the country, and you'll suit us."

This did not please Mikhailov, who tried to put in an argument against there being any leader, but he was overruled, one of the men even turning to him with: "You, in particular, need to be careful. Don't be too anxious to shoot when you first catch sight of the tiger. Wait until you can aim directly at his head or heart. If you don't, he'll teach you something that you'll never forget in this life."

"Keep your counsel for your own use," retorted Mikhailov. "I don't need it."

Father here raised a warning hand and began to assign to each one present his place and duty.

"You, Simeon," he said, turning to one, "take the hounds along the low places of the valley, so as to get the tiger to move out of the bushes into the open spaces in the hills. You, Ivan and Feodor, take your places on the western side of the brush and keep close watch. Don't let the beast escape into the forest. And you, Mikhailov, and you, Foma, remain as quiet as dead men on the left side of the brush, about one hundred feet apart. Mind, you're to hide in the tall grass and not show yourselves. The tiger will probably try to run to Hog Valley. Don't miss him. Be vigilant and brave."

Then he turned to me. "As for you, Vanka, stay with Granny under the oak on yonder hill. Tie the horses well and see that they don't get frightened at either the tiger or the shots. See that you don't stare open-mouthed at the sky and don't go where you're not wanted. If you leave your place — you'll be sorry that the tiger didn't get you. Do you understand?"

Something in my father's voice cheered me. I felt that he knew what he was about and that I must obey.

Then Mikhailov asked father, "Where are you going?"

"To the north of the valley, where I'll take the rest and station them." Turning to Simeon he added, "Don't let the hunt commence until you hear a shot from my rifle." And, followed by several men, he left us.

Before those remaining separated, I heard Mikhailov remark to his neighbor, "Oh, he's foxy. He's selected the best place for himself. We'll not even catch a glimpse of the tiger."

Here Daria turned quickly to him with, "You've returned from service as big a fool as when you left. Do your duty and you'll find that Alexis Pavlovitch has done you justice." Striking her horses with a whip, Daria started for the oak. I followed.

When I had tied the horses, I tried to wait patiently for day-break. But oh, how long the hours seemed! My fingers grew stiff with the frost. I tried to limber them up by blowing on them after I had taken off my mittens. Here Daria jumped to the ground, picked up a big handful of snow and rubbed her fingers with it. After wiping them she put them into the big sleeves of her fur coat, saying, "Now even my old fingers are warm. Follow my example."

I bent down, my fingers so stiff that I could hardly grab up any snow. As I rubbed them, their flexibility gradually returned, and I dried them on the border of my fur coat. Then, still imitating my companion, I put them into my sleeves. They felt as warm as if they had just come out of boiling water.

By the time the first glimmer of dawn appeared, I could already distinguish Mikhailov, who was lying half hidden in the dry grass, and a moment after, the dogs leaping around Simeon, who tried to keep them quiet while waiting for my father's signal.

Just before sunrise, the faint sound of a shot from down the valley came to us. Daria awakened from her doze. At the same time the hounds commenced to bark and move toward the dry snow-covered brush covering the bottom of the valley. At first Simeon held them tightly by a rope and they barked regularly and carelessly. Soon, however, there was a change. Anger and hate mingled with their bark.

"They have scented the tiger," whispered Daria.

I forgot everything, horses, mule, myself, as I stared fearfully into the snow-covered underbrush for a glimpse of the beast. At first I could see nothing, for the white covering grew blinding under the first rays of the sun. That and the yellow leaves of the low Mongolian oaks hid Simeon, the hounds, and the tiger, making it seem a wall of mystery to me.

I shivered for fear of the men as I recalled how easily this tiger had carried off our cow. It was not until later that I learned that even the most ferocious of wild creatures will avoid meeting man unless forced to do so.

The sun rose just behind where I was stationed, and gradually I could see two stationary black spots against the white of the hills opposite. They were Ivan and Feodor.

On our side, Mikhailov and Foma showed more excitement. They even kept bobbing into sight, despite my father's strict orders to remain hidden. I also made out two Cossacks, mere specks, down in the valley. But nowhere could I find my father.

Suddenly I noticed a movement in the brush some distance away. I thought it must be Simeon and his hounds, until an open space was reached and I distinctly saw an animal apparently the size of a mouse. Unable to control myself I cried: "The tiger!"

Daria's hand instantly covered my mouth. But Mikhailov had heard and signaled "Where?"

I tried to show him as best I could without turning my eyes from the tiny spot on the snow. It may have been that the tiger heard my loud exclamation; it may have been that something else attracted his attention; in any case he remained motionless for a few seconds. Then with one leap he disappeared again into the brush.

Shortly after, Simeon and the two hounds appeared in the same spot. Then my excitement cannot be described as I saw the tiger run exactly toward where Mikhailov was concealed. From my elevated position all this was visible; Mikhailov, however, could not see how close the tiger was to him.

In a very short time the beast had reached the eastern side. He appeared so unexpectedly before Mikhailov that the latter, instead of shooting, uttered a curse, and the tiger turned back. Here Mikhailov committed the grave error against which he had been warned. He shot in the direction that the tiger had gone and evidently hit without killing him.

A terrible roar followed as the creature turned and jumped right on the man who had wounded him.

CHAPTER X

THE HUNT—CONTINUED

My heart gave a wild leap and I grabbed hold of the side of the sled for support. Then a great many things happened, but I recall them to the smallest detail.

As the tiger's roar rang out, all the horses tied to the trees and in my care broke their halters and rushed wildly away. Daria's two horses attached to the sled, followed, leaping over all obstacles. Daria's greatest efforts were powerless to even reduce their speed. I soon forgot all about them, however, so intent did I become on the picture before me.

I saw Foma, who was nearest, make a few jumps toward him and then kneel and point his rifle at the beast who clung to Mikhailov. A shot followed. Immediately after, the tiger turned, looking just like a big cat. He gave three or four convulsive shakes and fell back without a sound on the snow, his hind legs sinking deep into it, and his front legs stretched to the sky.

I ran toward Mikhailov, but, before I reached him, I felt a strong arm on my neck and a voice interrupted by deep breathing: "Stop, you crazy boy! Wait! He might be able to break your neck yet. A tiger doesn't die as quickly as that." I stopped, and with the man who had spoken gazed where the tiger lay. It remained motionless. After a few seconds my companion judged it safe to approach. Foma had shot him in the ear, killing him instantly.

Mikhailov was lying with his right side and part of his head deeply imbedded in the snow. His fur coat had been torn from his shoulder, revealing a deep wound from which the shoulder blade projected. At first sight his head seemed attached to the body only by a shred of skin, so unnaturally was it twisted to one side and covered by a thick mass of blood.

Though shivering as if with a fever, I could not turn my eyes from the terrible sight. I regained possession of myself only when I heard my father's voice as he came up on horseback.

As he jumped down to examine Mikhailov he turned saying, "Go, help my brother catch Daria's horses."

The man addressed leaped at once on father's horse and hit it with a nagaika (a Cossack whip). The spirited animal put back its ears, and like an arrow shot out toward where Daria's horses could be just seen running around in circles in the snow.

One by one the other hunters arrived and stood around Mikhailov. No one seemed to know what to do, and no one dared, apparently, say what he thought, although two of the men took off their hats as is generally done in the presence of Death.

Finally some one did turn to my father with, "Is he quite dead?"

As if in answer, Mikhailov just then made a faint movement with a finger of his left hand. It seemed to me that he was trying to signify something by this, especially as it was followed by a slight moan or two. Then again there was silence.

Here some of the men began to talk, wondering how he could have made so great a blunder. My father stopped them. "It's time to do something," he said, and beckoning to two others to help him, tried to raise the wounded man into a more comfortable position. Mikhailov groaned faintly.

"Better let him die without hurting him," interjected my uncle, turning his head away.

"But look!" quickly exclaimed an intelligent-looking young man. "His face isn't injured at all. Only his neck is torn. He might live long enough to take the sacrament at least, and even, perhaps, make his last will."

Four of the men again raised Mikhailov, my father supporting his head, and placed him on a saddle blanket that had been stretched out on the snow.

Meanwhile Daria's horses had been caught and she had driven up. As soon as sufficiently near, she slipped down from her sleigh and tottered toward the wounded man. Blood was still dripping from the neck.

"Fools!" she exclaimed, looking indignantly at the men. "It's lucky the blood has partially clogged or he would have bled to death before your eyes."

Then turning to one of the Cossacks she added: "Your blouse looks clean. Give it to me."

Without a word the man took it off and handed it to her.

Paying no attention to the bits of advice that now began to be given, such as "Put some tobacco on the torn place," "Powder is the best thing," she tore the shirt into pieces and began to bandage the wound.

I watched her quick, sure movements with a constantly growing admiration, my former liking for her changing to a sort of reverent love.

When she had finished and stretched herself with difficulty, I found that the men had not been idle. Dried twigs had been spread in the sleigh and these covered with several horse-blankets, the whole forming a comfortable bed. The quickness with which it had been made showed that the Cossacks were used to needing it.

Several Cossacks now lifted the wounded man on to the sleigh with as great care and skill as that possessed by the best trained nurses. They then helped Daria to an especially prepared place by his side. My uncle took the driver's seat, and I, without waiting for invitation or permission, jumped up next to him. Slowly we drove off.

I looked back once or twice to see what those left behind were doing. Some of them hung the tiger to a strong tree, the skin having already been loosened from his legs. Then they carefully cut the thin under skin with their hunting knives and gradually pulled it off from the tail down.

As soon as we arrived at the village, a man was sent on the swiftest horse to be found, to the nearest stannica (an administrative Cossack station) where a doctor was to be found.

It was not until late at night that the doctor arrived. When he had examined the wound, he said: "I can't understand how he has lasted so long with so little help."

"Will he live?" some one asked.

The doctor shook his head. "There's but little chance of that," he said.

But I may as well say here that Mikhailov did live, his wonderful constitution pulling him through. His neck, however, was crippled, his head always inclining toward the left side, and his left arm practically disabled. The accident taught him wisdom, and later he took to hunting again, becoming the most renowned hunter of wolves and bears in our district.

The tiger skin was sold to a passing merchant for sixty rubles, while the tiger's heart was bought by a Chinaman, who intended, it was said, to reduce it to powder and sell it to those who thought that they could thus have some of the tiger's bravery transmitted to them. The skull was given to Daria in acknowledgment of her services, and kept by her, with many other very curious things, in the front room of her little log house.

CHAPTER XI

A JOURNEY

One day, not long after a traveling merchant had brought us news of Dimitri, my father called me to the bench on which he sat, and putting his hands on my head, asked: "How would you like to learn to read and write?"

At first I did not know what to answer, the question was so unexpected. Glancing at my mother, I saw that it made her so uneasy that she dropped a tumbler on the floor, a very unusual happening.

Although father did not insist on my answering, the question kept coming back to me all that day and the next, until I decided that to learn to read and write would be a very good thing.

For some days following this question, I noticed that father seemed to be brooding over something, and finally, to my great surprise, I accidentally learned that I was the cause of his worry.

One night after I had gone to my bed, where I lay dreaming of having won distinction in the army, I heard mother say, "What's worrying you, Alexis? Are you sick? Or is anything wrong with the horses? Or"—here her voice trembled—"have you had bad tidings of Dimitri that you're afraid to tell me?"

"Oh, no," father answered. "Nothing is wrong." Then he abruptly changed the conversation. "Do you remember Mongalov?"

"Do you mean your chum, Vanka, whom my mother spanked when he threw mud at me as a child?"

"That's the one," replied my father. "But you mustn't call him Vanka any more. Didn't Mitya tell you that he is now a sotnik?"

"What! An officer! Is it possible?"

"Yes,—and I am not," said my father with a certain bitterness in his voice. "Yet I had a better chance in some ways than he." Here his voice sank lower. "Now, our Vanka isn't stupid, and if we give him an education I don't see why he shouldn't become an officer. Too bad that that fellow

Gabrilov, whom we had here as a teacher last spring, turned out to be such a drunkard. We really had to get rid of him."

Mother interrupted him. "Judging by Gabrilov, education isn't such a splendid thing. Boys brought up in town learn all sorts of wicked things. I'd rather keep Vanka here. He can learn to be as good a Cossack in our village as anywhere else. Mongalov may dress better than you, but he isn't respected a bit more. After Katia is married I don't see how I can get along without Vanka."

Here I fell asleep with the pleasant knowledge that, after all, I was not simply a nuisance but meant something to my parents.

The next morning father went about his work as usual, feeding the horses and cattle, and bringing wood and cutting it. In the meantime mother brought water from the well in the middle of the yard, and I pumped water into a big trough to which I led the horses.

When this had been done, father caught two of the horses, gave them some grain and tied them to a post.

Seeing my look of inquiry, he smilingly repeated a favorite proverb, "Don't try to learn too much or your hair will turn gray."

As we went in to breakfast his lips moved as if he were talking to himself, a habit he had formed whenever he had a great deal on hismind. Mother watched him with a troubled air, and at last asked: "What's the matter, Alexis?"

Without replying to her question, he said, "I have to go to Habarovsk to-day, and I'll take Vanyuska with me. I've been promising him the ride for a long time."

I jumped up, waved my arms, and with my mouth full of bread, shouted: "Hurrah!"

My mother stopped me. "Sit down, you foolish boy. You can't go. I need you."

But, after a long argument, mother agreed to my going. Then father and I cleaned the horses and tied their tails up as high as possible, for at this time of the year the roads were very muddy. I placed a light saddle on the horse I was to ride, and father's military saddle with its high trees on the other horse. As father put some sacks with forage behind these, Katia came out with something that mother was sending Dimitri. I was very glad to see this, for it meant that we were going to visit the Cossack barracks.

Half an hour later we had left home and were making our way through the deep mud. It was a beautiful Spring morning. The air was fresh and clear, and, despite the heavy road, the horses were full of spirit and went on with a light and springy gait.

At a turn of the road I suddenly saw two rabbits sitting about a hundred feet from us. Pointing to them, I called to my father to look. Here my horse jumped to one side and I was all but thrown from the saddle.

My father was quite angry. He turned to me exclaiming roughly: "What's the matter with you? A Cossack should always watch his horse. He must never be taken by surprise even should the horse leap a fence. You almost fell like a sack."

Since that lesson I have never failed in watchfulness, never "fallen asleep," as the Cossacks say, even when trying to ride a mule or an ox.

We did not meet many travelers. Once a company of dusky, flat-featured natives of the Lake Baikal region, passed us, splendidly mounted on their horses. Their large, squat bodies gave them a somewhat forbidding air, but I knew how peaceful and harmless they really are. The Russians call them Bratskie (brotherly people). One was dressed in a long, purplish blue cloak, lined with fur, and had on a curious blue cone-shaped hat. The others were evidently Cossacks, for they had on the distinguishing uniform. They may have been on their way to some Buddhist shrine, for the Russian Government, severe with its own people, allows those born into other religions to worship as they please. "God gave us our religion. He gave them theirs," expresses the attitude taken.

It was just here that we were overtaken by a man mounted like ourselves on a shaggy Siberian pony. When he had come up, both he and my father gave expression to surprised greetings. He proved to be an old-time acquaintance. There was no end of questions and answers for he rode with us as far as our destination. He had just come from the city of Vladivostok, the great growing seaport of Siberia. As he gave a glowing description of the place, I was reminded of the meaning of the name Vladi-vostok—possessor of the East.

"We may build a great trade with the United States through Vladivostok," he remarked among other things. "It has a splendid, land-locked harbor, large enough for any number of vessels,—and a beautiful one as well."

"But isn't it frozen a large part of the year?" my father asked.

"From the latter part of December to April. It's really too bad so great a country as ours hasn't an outlet further south. But all trade isn't stopped on account of the ice. There is a channel kept open for the largest ships all winter by means of ice-breakers."

"What kind of people are there in Vladivostok?" I ventured to ask, half fearful of saying something ridiculous.

The man turned to me with a smile. "Many exactly like those in your village. Then people from different parts of Europe, and Chinese and Japanese. Also quite a number of Koreans, whom you can tell by their white dress. You'll see those in Habarovsk, also." After a moment's pause, he went on, "The bay is called the Golden Horn (Zolotoy Rog). The town rises up from it in terraces. It is very picturesque."

"I suppose there is a fort there," I again ventured.

This time the man laughed. "If you visited this seaport you might think it all forts. There are defenses,—forts and guns,—whole lines of them, everywhere. The greater part of the population consists of soldiers and sailors."

Here my father broached the subject of which his mind seemed so full these days. "I suppose there are fine schools," he said.

I was so stiff by this time, and my back ached so much from the long unusual ride, that I was no longer able to concentrate my mind on anything except that I must not disgrace my father and myself by showing fatigue.

At last we approached the great Amur River. Across it we could just make out a few black spots and the shining roof of a church.

After a half hour ride we came to a place on the bank where a raft was stationed. A few people were already aboard, desiring, like ourselves, to be taken across. Two soldiers had the boat in charge, and as soon as we were on, every one helped them in making the somewhat difficult trip.

On the opposite bank we parted from our companion, and then, for the first time, I fully realized that we had reached our destination, — the important garrison town of Habarovsk.

CHAPTER XII

A GARRISON TOWN

This was my first visit to a city, and I gazed with very wide wonder at the wooden sidewalks, the big stores, the many two-story houses, the well-dressed women and the numerous soldiers on the street. I could hardly understand what father said to me, so absorbed was I in the entirely new scenes before me.

Suddenly we heard the sound of trumpets, cymbals, and tambourines, accompanied by a lively song. Then a company of Cossacks on horseback issued from a side street. At the head of the column rode a group of special singers, — pesenniki.

Father and I stationed ourselves near the edge of the street, and tried to find a familiar figure. The long row of faces splashed hereand there with mud; the similar uniforms, with rifles protruding from leather straps at the back and swords at the side; the hats tipped to the right, all exactly at the same angle; every left hand holding the bridle reins, every right hand placed on the hips; — how was it possible to distinguish among them?

I soon decided that my only chance of finding Dimitri was to look for his horse, which I knew to be gray, while the majority were bay. It was not long before I shouted: "Father, look at the eighth row! Dimitri!" Then still louder: "Dimitri! Dimitri! Look! Here we are!"

Brother turned and nodded, but, to my great astonishment, did not come to us, but followed the others without giving any other expression of recognition.

Then I heard father saying, "Why can't you be quiet? Dimitri can't come to us until his company is dismissed."

Meanwhile the Cossacks, six abreast, continued to ride past us whistling and singing.

The entire population of the place now seemed to gather on the sidewalk. There were merchants in front of their stores, boys who tried hard to keep step with the horses, women returning from market with baskets on their arms, all gazing with appreciation at what was a daily sight. How very desirable it seemed to me to be one of such a company. How glad I was that my brother belonged to it, and that my father was a Cossack. Hoping to impress a pretty little girl who stood near me, I took off my felt cap with its yellow cloth top, symbolic of the East Siberian Cossacks, and then having looked at it, slowly put it on again.

The Cossack officers rode on one side of the men. They were distinguished not only by their brighter uniforms but also by the half Arabian horses on which they were mounted. Many of them had silver-plated belts around their waists. They had no rifles, only swords that shone brightly, while revolvers hung from their left sides. The bridles of their horses glimmered with silver. All the horses were covered with foam, showing that the drill had been no easy one.

When we reached the barracks, the commanding officer gave an order, and the whole company leaped like one man from their horses to the ground. Another order, and the horses were led to the stables, adobe buildings covered with thatched roofs.

After the horses were rubbed down and fed, Dimitri at last came and embraced us, saying: "Wait for me at the rooms of the second platoon, where I'll join you as soon as I am free."

Then he ran with others to wash before taking his place in the dining-room. As we made our way to the dormitory, my attention was again attracted by singing, but of a different kind. It was the solemn prayer which was always chanted before dinner.

Soon we found ourselves in a long room in a brick building. Everything about it was exceedingly neat. High windows admitted plenty of light, and as all were open there was a fine circulation of fresh air. The walls were apparently freshly white-washed, the floors painted. In one corner hung a big ikon with a lamp under it. About fifty iron beds placed in two rows were down the middle. Each bed was covered with a gray blanket and each was marked with the name of the owner. Along the inside of the wall stood racks for the rifles.

When, after a half hour, we heard the chanting of the prayer of thanks in the dining-room near by, we looked expectantly at the door. The company soon filed in. Some stretched themselves on their beds, some sat down to read, and some began to mend their clothes.

When Dimitri came, one of father's first inquiries was regarding schools and the promotion to officer rank. My brother was not well posted and so called the sergeant-major to help him. Time passed quickly until the hour for drill. Then the first Cossack who noticed that an officer had entered the room, exclaimed, "Silence! Rise!"

At once there was deep quiet as all arose. I was amazed at the sudden change, and looked with respect and fear at the man who could produce it. It was father's old-time friend, Captain Mongalov. I watched everything that he did with great intentness, noted how his worn-out uniform was tightly buttoned, how erect he held his body. Even the curves of his legs, probably caused from living so much on horseback, and the way he swayed from side to side as he walked, attracted me. And how splendid and fierce I thought his big black mustache reaching almost to his ears.

His face was a peculiar mixture of the Russian and Asiatic types, occasionally met among Siberian Cossacks. When he smiled, he showed two rows of perfect ivory, and he smiled often. Yet even with his comrades his expression could change to one of great sternness at the least break of discipline.

When he saw us he turned to my father with, "From where do you hail, friend?"

Father slowly and smilingly replied, "Don't you recognize me, Ivan Petrovitch? I have just come from the Ussuri."

"What! Is it you, Alexis Pavlovitch!" Mongalov exclaimed. "It's ages since I last saw you." And he embraced my father.

After a short exchange of reminiscences, he turned to me. "Is this your son? He promises to make a fine Cossack! Are you keeping in mind, my son, Cossack ideals of bravery and honor?"

Drawing myself to my full height in imitation of the bearing of those around me, I answered as well as I could, looking straight into his eyes as I did so.

"Good!" he exclaimed, and taking hold of me under the elbows he tossed me, like an old acquaintance, high into the air.

Then, suddenly, he turned to my father. "You must excuse me now. I want to see more of you some evening at my house." And, in a flash, the genial friend had changed into the stern commander of a company who, at a single word from him, proceeded to do the various tasks necessary before retiring.

CHAPTER XIII

A COSSACK DRILL

The night was spent at the home of an aunt, whose husband, a grocer, was also a retired Cossack. Their home was a very humble one, but what it lacked in luxury it made up in the hospitality of its owners.

Fresh straw for beds was brought in and put in a room set apart. This straw was covered with heavy home-spun bed linen, some feather pillows, and two big fur coats as comforters. After a fire had been kindled in the stove, we were invited to partake of supper, which consisted of deer meat, pancakes heavily buttered, and sour cream.

After eating very heartily I became so sleepy that I was ordered to bed. When I awoke, the sun was streaming directly into my face.Father, who was already dressed, tried to hurry me by saying, "You are a nice Cossack! They must be half through the drill which you were so anxious to see. Mongalov has promised to give you a horse so that you can follow the sotnia" (a company of from one hundred and twenty to one hundred and sixty horsemen).

This was news to me. Burning my mouth in my haste to swallow my hot tea, I was ready to follow my father in a few minutes.

When we came to the barracks the Cossacks, holding on to the reins of their horses with their right hands, were assembled in the front yard, and the sergeant-major was calling the roll. "We came too late for the morning prayer," my father whispered to me as the roll was ended.

Here came an order from the sergeant-major. "Seat yourselves." At once every man leaped upon his horse.

"Line up," came next, and the horses arranged themselves in two straight lines, head to head and breast to breast.

"Silence!" was the next order, and all gazed mutely ahead, immovable as statues.

Some long command, the words of which I did not catch, followed, and the company changed positions to six in a row. A moment after, all were trotting along the road out of town.

As we started to follow, the sergeant-major hailed me. "Good morning! Are you the young fellow whom Captain Mongalov wishes to have a horse?"

"Yes," answered my father for me, adding, "But I'm afraid he isn't a good enough rider to follow the company."

"Never fear," returned the sergeant-major. "I'll bet he's a true Cossack and will take to horses as a duck does to a lake."

A soldier now held a horse until I had climbed into its saddle. When he let it go, it started so fast to catch up with the others that I had difficulty in keeping my seat. However I did this, and also managed to prevent the horse from joining the ranks.

After we had left the city, the company was halted in a big plain which stretched far out before us. It was somewhat rolling, with here and there washed-out places. The sergeant-major rode along the line inspecting the ammunition and appearance of the men. While he was doing this, horses were heard approaching at full speed. On the foremost sat Mongalov. A little behind came two other officers.

"Greetings to you, little brothers!" he shouted as he rode along the line without reining in his horse.

Then I was almost dumbfounded by the suddenness of a gigantic answer. "Good Day to Your Honor," came from the company as from one man.

Mongalov noticed me and kindly stopped to say: "Keep close to the trumpeter and you'll see everything. Only don't get into anybody's way or I'll have to arrest you." With a smiling nod he rode to the front.

At a word from him, the officers took their places. Then followed several changes of position, all done with great rapidity and precision. I learned later that Captain Mongalov's men were unusually well trained even for Cossacks. The Captain loved his profession and the men were devoted to him. There was something fatherly in the great care that he took of the

Cossacks under him. On the other hand, he was severe in punishing any breach of discipline. No one resented this since he was just and endeavored to make the punishment corrective.

At the conclusion of the drill Mongalov called out in a voice resounding with warm approval: "Well done, little brothers, well done. Thank you!"

And again, as one man, the company responded: "We were glad to do our best, Your Honor."

"Down!" was the next order.

All leaped together to the ground.

"Rest and smoke," came again, and he and his officers jumped off their own horses and stood together discussing the next drill.

The company followed their example, and soon burst into loud talk and laughter, while clouds of smoke arose from pipes and cigarettes.

In the meantime I didn't know what to do. I was afraid that if I climbed down I couldn't get up again on my horse, who seemed unusually lively and disobedient to me. But I was not left long in this awkward position, for after a quarter of an hour of rest the Cossacks were again on their horses, every man ready to obey any order.

To judge by the alert look on their faces, the most important part of the drill was now to come. Every eye was turned toward their commanding officer as if trying to guess what new trick would be required of them.

Mongalov sat on his steed, his right hand twirling his mustache, his eyes directed far down the field as if surveying the distance or estimating the difficulties before his men. Then his voice rang out abruptly: "Company, build lava!"

These words produced an effect like a discharge of ammunition in the midst of the Cossacks. The horses rushed madly forward and to each side of the center, forming a kind of fan. Only by putting forth the full strength of my arm did I keep my horse in place, the proud animal trying so hard to show that she understood the command.

In the wink of an eye the compact body of horses was transformed into a long line of separate riders, stretched so that there was abouttwenty feet between each. All were still, the men with swords drawn out of their scabbards.

Mongalov no longer shouted orders but indicated what was to be done by waving his sword in different directions. As if charmed by its motions, the long line moved, now to the right, now to the left, now forward, now backward.

Once Mongalov, evidently dissatisfied, ordered the trumpeter to repeat through the trumpet the order given with the sword. Since that time I have loved the harmonious sounds of the Cossack trumpet which in a very short time I grew to understand as plainly as spoken words.

Here something happened. Mongalov again made a sign to the trumpeter. A short, disagreeably false tone was the result. At this the Cossacks acted like mad. With swords outstretched, they bent down to their horses' manes and with a terrible yell, "Whee-ee!" they rushed wildly to the front against an imaginary enemy. My horse with ears back, took her bit between her teeth, and flew after them. Here I learned how rapidly a horse can travel. The air whistled in my ears; my hat was blown off; my feet flew from the stirrups; and not to be thrown off, I grabbed the horse by the mane, uttering a short prayer.

I did not know what was happening around me until I found myself, perhaps because of my light weight, among the other Cossacks. Around me were excited faces with wild expressions; faces that had lost their humanity; faces such as demons might possess, or Christian fanatics who would lay down their lives for their faith.

As we rode, a big washout suddenly loomed before us. Most of the horses immediately jumped over and disappeared in a mad rush forward. But my horse and those of three men, perhaps through some fault on our part, did not make the proper jump. I felt a shock as the hoofs of my horse struck the opposite banks of the ravine, and then the horse fell to the ground, throwing me over its head into the middle of a mud-hole.

As I struggled to get up, there came a new signal of three long harmonious sounds. The lava was stopped. Once out of the hole, I saw a line of still excited horses far to the front. Two or three riderless horses, one of them mine, were running around them. Not far from me lay another breathing hard and trying vainly to rise. Near it a Cossack lay stretched out, while two others sat on the ground a short distance away.

In a short time Mongalov, the trumpeter, and two officers, came galloping to us. His first question was to me. "Are you hurt?"

"No," I replied, in a voice that sounded strange to me, so shaken was I with the new experience.

"Here," said Mongalov to a Cossack, "place this boy back of yourself." Then, throwing the reins of his horse to the trumpeter, he leaped down and turned his attention to the man lying stretched on the ground.

He proved to be alive but with a leg broken and was put into the ambulance which had come up. "What's the matter with you?" Mongalov asked the two bruised, scratched, and mud-covered men who sat on the ground.

"Nichevo," they answered, smiling and shaking their heads. And as soon as their horses were caught and brought to them, they managed to leap on them as if in reality nothing had happened.

When my horse was led up, Mongalov looked at me where I sat ashamed to meet his gaze, holding tightly to the belt of the man before me. "You can stay where you are, my boy," he said kindly, "or ride your own horse. But let me congratulate you on being now a trueCossack. The man who has never fallen from his saddle can never make a satisfactory cavalryman!"

How much good these words did me! They not only made me feel at ease with myself, but taught me one of the best lessons of my life: that mistakes or mishaps do not down a man who can rise above them. With some difficulty I slipped from my safe position, and climbed as swiftly as possible into the saddle of my former horse.

It was not long before the entire company were again on their way back to town. At the call "Singers forward," several Cossacks left the ranks and took their places at the head of the column. One of these men was urged to sing and he responded with a Little Russian song about a Cossack who returned home from fighting the Turks. At the conclusion of each stanza those surrounding the soloist began the refrain which was taken up by the entire company. Listening to this story-telling song I almost forgot that I was in Siberia, so vividly did pictures of what took place far away a hundred years ago pass before me.

This song was followed by a boisterous rollicking one. The chorus was loud and accompanied by cymbals and tambourine. Any one glancing at the broadly smiling and yelling faces, would not have believed that their owners were just returning from the most strenuous kind of work, had it not been for the mud and perspiration visible and their foam-covered horses.

CHAPTER XIV

AN EVENING VISIT

As we approached the town, there was less talking and laughing and the singing became less boisterous. The crowds gathered as I had seen them before, and showed their appreciation of the songs by now and then joining in the chorus.

Before the barracks were reached, the men leaped down from the horses, loosened their saddle girths, and led them to the stables. Here they unsaddled them, gave them hay, and curried them, while the non-commissioned officers inspected their legs as well as the skin that had been under the saddles. This was done with much caution, for Captain Mongalov was particularly strict regarding the health and care of the horses. Where there was negligence, his usual reprimand was apt to end with: "Don't forget next time that the Cossack army's efficiency depends more on the sound legs of a good horse than on the blockhead who does not know enough to take care of them."

When all the horses had been inspected, cleaned, watered, and given their prescribed measure of oats, the men were allowed to go to get themselves ready for dinner, leaving, however, four men whose turn it was to take care of the stables.

I wish there were time to tell of all the wonders of that garrison visit, of the dinner in the big dining-room with Dimitri, of the lessons given the young men, of the instructing officers, and most of all of my first sight of the fascinating and difficult exercise called the jigatovka, which I saw that same afternoon, and which consisted of horse vaulting, dart throwing at a gallop and many other things.

Captain Mongalov invited us all to spend the evening at his house, and by six o'clock my father, my aunt, and I were at his front door. Being a little in advance of the others, I tried to open it, but, to my surprise, found it was not possible to do so. Could it be locked, I wondered. In our village such a thing was never done except under very unusual circumstances. Father, noting my surprise, pointed to a handle on the door which he bade me pull down. I did so and heard a loud ring within. In a moment the door was opened by an orderly, who greeted us like friends and invited us in.

When he had gone to announce us, I glanced around the room. A big desk occupied the left corner, the top of which was covered with books relating to military regulations. The big brass inkstand with its two kinds of ink, black and red, especially attracted me. On a table near by, a heavy nickel-plated lamp threw its light over a mass of official papers. Instead of benches around the room as at my own home there were numerous comfortable chairs.

One wall was covered with the skins of wild beasts. I recognized those of a black and of a brown bear. Above these were fastened enormous antlers. On their very numerous branches hung swords, daggers, and other arms. Pictures, one of which was that of an old lady plainly dressed (the Captain's mother), hung on the opposite wall.

Then my attention fastened itself on a big tiger skin covering a sofa. I touched the artificial eyes which looked so intently at me; I wondered if the teeth were real. So occupied did I become that it was like an electric shock to feel a sudden clap on my shoulder and the Captain's hearty voice greeting me.

I immediately experienced a strong desire to converse with him as I would with an older brother, but he had turned from me and wasbusy answering some of my father's numerous questions.

The bell rang again and admitted a new group. My aunt at once stepped up and threw her arms about one of the women in it, who proved to be her own cousin from the pretty neighboring city of Blagovestchensk. Closely following the cousin came her husband, a former artillery officer, with a very long beard. His thick, bushy gray hair framed a small sympathetic face. With them was a pale but very attractive lady dressed in a gray suit. A little girl of about my own age, had hold of her hand.

Mongalov greeted this lady with particular respect and gallantly kissed her hand. Then he invited all to take off their wraps and make themselves at home, that is, all but Nina, the little girl, and myself. He had beckoned to us to follow the orderly into the garden.

Here we found many things to interest us. There was a horse that refused sugar from Nina but accepted, to my great delight, bread and salt from me. There were fancy chickens, and, best of all, a sort of see-saw on which I condescended to accept Nina's invitation to play. We stood as straight as possible on the board which was balanced on a log, and as it went up and down jumped alternately into the air, each time going a little higher. Nina was not at all afraid, and despite a peculiar seriousness about her, we were well acquainted when supper was announced.

The table, set with more good things than I had ever seen before, was in a long dining-room. Soon everybody was laughing and joking, everybody except Nina's mother. It seemed to me that she was not like the rest of us but I could not have told why.

The supper lasted a long time and when we returned to the big living-room, the piano, which stood on one side, was opened and Lidia Ivanovna, the lady in gray, consented to play some Russian airs from Glinka's opera, "Life of the Tzar."

Shortly after, both she and her little daughter as well as my aunt's cousin left, pleading the weariness still felt by the strangers from long travel.

When they had gone, Mongalov turned to the former artillery officer, whose name was Kuzmin, and asked, "Where did you meet Lidia Ivanovna?"

"She came with a caravan of prisoners sent from St. Petersburg." (Petrograd.) "I am told that she is looking for her husband who was sent to Siberia a few years ago as a political exile. If she can find him, she wishes to share his fate."

Here I exclaimed impulsively: "It ought to be easy to find him. The government officials can surely tell her where he is."

Kuzmin smiled bitterly. "They can, perhaps, if they wish. You must remember, however, that Siberia is no little state. When I came here, it was with many thousands of prisoners, mostly Poles who had fought for their country's independence, and they are now so scattered that you might not meet a dozen in a lifetime."

"How big is Siberia?" I asked.

"In figures, it is more than five million square miles, but see that map hanging on the wall," said the old man with some eagerness, as if glad of the change in the conversation, "and see that little dot. That stands for the biggest city you know, the one you are now in, Habarovsk."

"That little dot!" I exclaimed in surprise, for no one had ever explained a map to me before.

"This waving line," continued Kuzmin, "is the Amur River."

Again I stared incredulously. How could a little line stand for the very wide Amur whose waters ran from horizon to horizon!

"Now that is only a small part of Siberia," said my new teacher. "From here at Habarovsk to the Ural Mountains, which separate Siberia from Russia, it takes two months to travel both day and night in a carriage."

"Tell me some other things about Siberia," I begged.

He pointed to a blue spot in the south. "This is Lake Baikal, the largest body of fresh water in Asia, about four hundred miles long and about forty-five miles wide. It is fifteen hundred feet above the level of the sea. It is a place full of mystery. I don't know if any one yet has been able to find how deep it is. On one side are all kinds of caverns and arches. It's pretty but it's mysterious. Now and then the earth in the vicinity trembles and quakes. Irkutsk, the largest and most important city in Siberia, is not very far from it."

After a moment's pause, he went on: "Let me tell you something of Blagovestchensk, my own city. But no; I'd talk too long. Why don't you move there?" turning suddenly to my father.

My father shook his head. "If I move," he said slowly, "I want to try farming."

"Farming offers many inducements," agreed Kuzmin. "I meet many farmers who came here penniless and now have hundreds of acresof land and hundreds of head of cattle and stables filled with grain."

"Were you ever in St. Petersburg?" I asked unexpectedly. At this question a queer change came over Kuzmin's face and he looked down without answering.

Here Mongalov reached for his balalaika, a sort of Russian mandolin, and began to play some gay Russian airs on it.

When we reached home, I asked my father why Kuzmin did not wish to talk about St. Petersburg.

"He is a useful and clever man," my father answered, "but, poor fellow, he belongs to the unfortunates."

From that I understood that, like Lidia Ivanovna's husband, the former artillery officer was an exile.

CHAPTER XV

LENT AND EASTER

Next morning my father took me to an exhibition held to show something of the resources of Siberia. While I studied the many evidences of great mineral wealth, my father devoted his attention to everything that pertained to farming.

On the way back to my aunt's I learned that we were not to go home yet, father having decided to stay for the week of repentance, a religious custom observed by orthodox Russians.

"You are now old enough to take your first sacrament after confession," he said to me.

When I went next to the big church, with its onion-shaped dome, I felt quite nervous thinking of all the faults and sins that I would have to confess for the first time in my life.

The service was a very solemn one. Every once in a while one of the black-robed priests came out from behind the sacred gates on the altar and read the prayer:

"Lord and Protector of my life,

Keep me from idleness,

Keep me from disappointment,

Keep me from false ambition,

Keep me from idle chattering.

Give me chastity,

Give me humility and love,

Me, Thy servant.

O Heavenly Czar, open my eyes to my sins;

Let me not judge my neighbors,

Let me reverence Thee always."

Not until the end of the service did the choir sing something very sweet in a minor key.

Child though I was, I left the church with a sense of the vanity of earthly things. I was ready to repent. I particularly remembered a day when I had taken a stick and hit my dog, poor dear Manjur. This, I told myself, I must confess, and also how often I had teased my baby sister.

On the night of confession, when, after a very long wait, my turn came, I found myself before a priest whose long beard made his face remind me of pictures of prophets that I had seen. It was very late, and he looked tired, but his eyes shone with sympathy as he listened to my brief recital.

I was so overcome with weariness when I reached home that I threw myself, supperless and partly dressed, on my bed and at once fell asleep.

I awoke very hungry next morning and after washing, hurried to the table where breakfast usually awaited me. The table was empty and all the people in the room were dressed in their Sunday clothes.

"Get ready quickly," said my father, "to come with us to church."

"But can't I have some bread and tea first?" I asked.

"No, indeed," said my father sternly. "You must not drink even a drop of water between confession and the taking of the sacrament."

"A drop of water!" I repeated in confusion. For it had happened that I had swallowed a drop when washing that morning. This troubled me until later the priest assured me that that did not count, since it had been involuntary.

I went to church with my stomach groaning for food. This, and the incense-laden air, caused me to feel faint until at last with many others, I received my share of the consecrated bread and wine.

This somewhat revived me, and I looked around with more interest at the people near by. There were several persons of note in the church, some in government uniforms with numerous medals on their breasts. Mongalov and his Cossack officers were among these, dressed in entirely new uniforms, but without fire-arms or ammunition, even their swords being detached and kept for them by outsiders until they had partaken of the sacrament.

When we came back to my aunt's I found many preparations already made for the Easter festival. The big dining-table had been much enlarged. It was covered with a white cloth and decorated with flowers and greens. On it were all kinds of attractive food. I was most impressed by what the Russians call pashka. It was in the shape of a pyramid and had been made by my aunt from cottage cheese, mixed with cream, sugar, and raisins. On it were figures of the Cross.

On each side of the pashka, which occupied the center of the table, was an entire ham baked in dough, several dozen eggs covered with various bright designs, and many other things.

To my great disappointment, nobody was allowed to touch even a bit of bread. Everything had to wait for Easter morn.

I was told that I should be awakened that night, and I was by the solemn ringing of the heaviest bells in the neighborhood. We dressed hastily and hurried to the church for the midnight service. There were so many already there that we had difficulty in entering.

Everybody looked happy, even the priests who were all dressed in white, silvery robes. When the service was over there was much kissing, every one repeating, "Christ is risen," or the response, "He is risen indeed."

It was almost four o'clock before we returned home with two or three guests who had been invited to break the fast with us. Before any other food was served, small pieces of consecrated pashka and an Easter cake called kulich were passed around.

The next day was spent by the men in paying calls to all whom they knew. As they had to eat and drink at every house, the result can be imagined.

The Easter celebration lasted a full week. What I liked best about it was the merry rolling of eggs down hill, the swings, enormous slides and see-saws, and other amusements provided for the children.

At last the joyous time came to an end, and after a last breakfast with Dimitri in the dining-room of the Second Platoon, father and I mounted our horses for home.

It seemed very long to me since I had come away. I thought several times of Peter and wondered if I could not show him some of the tricks of the jigatovka. When we neared our village, I sat very proud and erect with my mind quite made up that mother would surely mistake me for Dimitri. But as we rode into our yard, instead of anything like that happening, mother came running out and throwing her arms about me exclaimed: "O Vanyuska, you must be tired out from your long ride. Come in quickly and tell me how you ever managed for so long without your mother?"

THE END